A B C D E F G H I J

MARC BROWN

D.W.'S GUIDE TO PRESCHOOL

SCHOLASTIC INC.

New York   Toronto   London   Auckland   Sydney
Mexico City   New Delhi   Hong Kong   Buenos Aires

*For Bonnie Walmsley,
a great sister and gifted teacher*

ISBN 0-439-40469-X

12 11 10 9 8 7 6 5 4 3 2 1   5 6 7 8 9/0

Printed in the U.S.A.   40

First Scholastic printing, September 2004

Welcome to my preschool!
I'm D.W.

The first thing we do is say good-bye to our parents. Some kids are sad, but I'm not. I love preschool! Besides, the parents come back when we're finished. It's no big deal.

We always start the day with hellos. I say hello to everybody, even our class pet, Speedy. He's a gerbil. Once, he got loose and Ms. Morgan screamed when she found him in her purse.

Gerbil Food

Ms. Morgan is our teacher. She fixes our boo-boos and gives us hugs. She smiles a lot. She's really nice.

Don't worry. We have bathroom breaks whenever we need them. Once, Dennis wet his pants. I pretended I didn't notice because we're learning to be polite.

During free play we have blocks, a sand table, puzzles, tools, a play kitchen, and a telephone, but you can't really call people on it. We also learn how to share. Sometimes the Tibble twins have trouble with sharing.

Circle time is so much fun! Ms. Morgan teaches us songs and games. Today we are learning "The Wheels on the Bus." I don't know why, because we can't take the bus until next year, when we're in kindergarten.

The babies on the bus go, Wah wah wah!"

They give us food at preschool, too. It's usually good.
My mom says I'm allowed one thing I don't have to eat.
My one thing is tomatoes. Today is Emily's birthday and
her mom brought in cupcakes!

On nice days we go outside to play. There are so many good things to do. I'm not kidding! We run and jump and swing and slide. We have to take turns. The Tibbles are working on that, too.

We learn numbers at preschool. I can count to seven.
Emily can count to ten. Tommy Tibble says he can count
to a hundred, but we've never heard him do it.

Before I got to preschool, I worried that we would have spelling tests like my brother, Arthur. But that was silly because we only learn letters in preschool. Sometimes I crack myself up!

When we go on field trips we have to pick partners so we don't get lost. I got lost at the supermarket once and the boss announced my name on the loudspeaker. I've been thinking about asking him to do it again sometime.

Back at school we have even more fun. Sometimes we plant seeds, make popcorn, make books, paint, play dress-up, or make stuff with clay. We make really nice presents for our parents, too. Preschoolers don't have a lot of money, you know.

Every day at story time, Ms. Morgan reads us books. So far I haven't found any books that are like tomatoes because I love them all. When story time is over, we all help clean up.

Look! I told you the parents would come back. We have to get our stuff from our cubbies. My name is on my cubby. Isn't that cool? The last thing I do is say good-bye to everyone, even Speedy!

Now we have to go home. But I'm not sad, because
I get to come back tomorrow!